DOLLAR STORE DANNY
and the Shampoo Shark Attack

An AudioCraft Publishing, Inc. book

This book is a work of fiction. Names, places, characters and incidents are used fictitiously, or are products of the author's very active imagination.

Book storage and warehouses provided by *Chillermania* ©
Indian River, Michigan

Dollar $tore Danny and the Shampoo Shark Attack
Copyright © 2018 by Johnathan Rand/AudioCraft Publishing, Inc.
ISBN: 978-1-893699-44-1

Librarians/Media Specialists:
PCIP/MARC records available **free of charge** at
www.americanchillers.com

Illustrations by Michal Jacot © 2018 AudioCraft Publishing, Inc.
Cover/interior layout and graphics design by Howard Roark

Printed in USA

The
Shampoo
Shark
Attack

VISIT CHILLERMANIA!

WORLD HEADQUARTERS FOR BOOKS BY JOHNATHAN RAND!

Visit the HOME for books by Johnathan Rand! Featuring books, hats, shirts, bookmarks and other cool stuff not available anywhere else in the world! Plus, watch the American Chillers website for news of special events and signings at *CHILLERMANIA!* with author Johnathan Rand! Located in northern lower Michigan, on I-75! Take exit 313 . . . then south 1 mile! For more info, call (231) 238-0338. And be afraid! Be veeeery afraaaaaaiiiid . . . .

Chapter One

On Friday afternoon, Danny and his mother went to the dollar store. His mother needed to buy a few things.

"Danny," his mother said. "Will you help me?"

"Yes," Danny said.

"I need you to find a bottle of shampoo," said his mother.

"Okay," Danny said.

"When you find it, bring it to me," said Danny's mother.

"I will," Danny promised.

His mother went one way.

Danny went the other way.

"Let's see," Danny said as he walked down the aisle. He looked up at a big sign that read:

SHAMPOO
THIS WAY

"Ah," Danny said. "Mom will be happy."

While Danny walked, he looked at the shelves. He found a bottle of shampoo. It was blue and gray.

"Here it is," he said out loud. "Mom will be happy."

He picked up the bottle of shampoo.

Something very odd happened.

The bottle of shampoo wiggled in his hand.

Danny was surprised. The plastic bottle of shampoo felt squishy.

The plastic bottle wiggled again, and fell out of Danny's hand. He tried to grab it. He missed, and it fell to the floor.

But another very strange thing happened.

The shampoo bottle did not hit the floor.

Instead, the floor turned into water!

The shampoo bottle was gone. Danny was now standing in water up to his ankles! His shoes and socks were soaked.

Danny could not believe it. He wondered where the water came from.

But what happened next was even worse . . . and very, very scary.

Chapter Two

The water at Danny's feet rose. Soon, it was up to his knees.

"My pants are getting soaked," said Danny.

Then, the water rose to his waist!

"Now my pants are *really* getting soaked!" Danny said.

He looked around.

The entire store was filled with water. Items drifted from the shelves and floated on the surface.

So, Danny did what any boy would do. He called for his mother.

"Mom!" he yelled. His voice echoed through the dollar store.

But there was no answer.

"Mom?" he called out again.

No answer.

He wondered where the water came from. He wondered where his mother was. He wondered what he was going to do.

He became very worried.

Then, he heard a swishing sound behind him.

He turned.

He gasped.

A giant fin was coming

toward him!

Danny knew that could only mean one thing:

He was about to be attacked by a shark!

Chapter Three

Danny knew he was in serious trouble. A shark was about to attack him, and there was nowhere he could go!

As the giant fin came toward him, Danny knew he had to get

away. He knew he would not be able to swim fast enough. The shark would gobble him up, for sure!

"I've got to get away!" Danny said.

Then, he had an idea. As quickly as he could, he reached for the shelf.

He pulled himself up.

He climbed to the next shelf. Then the next.

But it was too late. The shark came out of the water. Danny could see rows and rows of very sharp teeth.

But strangest of all: the shark wasn't really a shark! It was the bottle of shampoo! Somehow, the bottle of shampoo had turned into a giant, man-eating shark!

Danny could only scream as the shampoo shark jumped out of the water and attacked.

Chapter Four

Danny closed his eyes and waited for the shark to gobble him up.

But the shark missed! He fell back into the water with a huge splash.

Danny was glad. But he was still very scared.

He saw the shark's fin slicing through the water.

"I made it out just in time," Danny said. "That shark almost gobbled me up!"

Still, Danny felt scared. He reached up to the next shelf. He wanted to climb higher. He wanted to get farther away from the shark.

But it was not to be.

His hand slipped, and Danny fell backwards. With a splash, he fell into the water.

And the shark was coming.

Chapter Five

Danny screamed, but he knew it would not help.

Quickly, he grabbed a shelf. The shark fin came closer. Using his legs and arms, Danny pulled himself up again.

The shark was still coming. Danny could see the giant fin slicing through the water.

He pulled himself higher.

The shark leapt from the water.

Danny screamed.

One of the shark's teeth caught the tail of Danny's shirt! The shark fell back into the water, pulling Danny with him!

For a moment, Danny was yanked underwater.

Danny was scared and confused. He swung his arms. He kicked his legs. Bubbles swirled before his eyes. He tried to grab something, anything.

And he did. He grabbed the only thing within reach.

The shark's fin.

As the shark began to swim, Danny swung his legs around him. He held fast to the fin, riding the shark like a horse as it swam through the dollar store!

Chapter Six

Danny was scared. He was on the back of a man-eating shark.

Or was it a bottle of shampoo?

Danny was not sure. It looked like a shark. But it also

looked like a giant bottle of shampoo.

Whatever it was, it had big, sharp teeth.

"Mom!" Danny screamed again. "Anybody! Help!"

Danny rode on the back of the shampoo shark. He held tightly to the fin, because he did not want to fall into the water. He did not want to be gobbled up by the shark.

Then, he heard a voice.

"Danny?"

It was his mother! She was somewhere in the dollar store!

"Watch out, Mom! There is a shark in the dollar store!"

The water began to drain away.

The shark began to shrink.

"Where are you?" Danny's mother said. Danny could not see his mom.

The shark became smaller. The water at his feet went away.

In seconds, Danny was seated on the dry floor. The water was gone. The shark was gone. The tile floor was dry. His clothing was dry.

In Danny's hands was an ordinary bottle of shampoo.

His mother came around the corner. She stopped and stared.

"There you are!" she said with a smile. "I have been looking all over for you."

"Mom!" Danny said. His eyes were wide. "There was water everywhere! The shampoo bottle turned into a shark! He tried to gobble me up!"

"Well," his mother said with a smile. "I'm glad he didn't. Come on. It's time to go. Bring the bottle of shampoo."

Danny's mother paid for their items, and they left the store.

"Didn't you see the shark?"

Danny asked his mom.

"No," Danny's mother replied.

"How about the water?" asked Danny.

Danny's mother smiled as they reached the car.

"No," she said. "I didn't see any water. But I'm glad we're safe."

"Me too," Danny said.

On the way home, he looked out the car window. He thought

about the shampoo bottle and how it had turned into a shark. He wondered what would happen the next time he and his mother visited the dollar store.

The End

Check out some of these chilling,

American Chillers:

#1: The Michigan Mega-Monsters
#2: Ogres of Ohio
#3: Florida Fog Phantoms
#4: New York Ninjas
#5: Terrible Tractors of Texas
#6: Invisible Iguanas of Illinois
#7: Wisconsin Werewolves
#8: Minnesota Mall Mannequins
#9: Iron Insects Invade Indiana
#10: Missouri Madhouse
#11: Poisonous Pythons Paralyze Pennsylvania
#12: Dangerous Dolls of Delaware
#13: Virtual Vampires of Vermont
#14: Creepy Condors of California
#15: Nebraska Nightcrawlers
#16: Alien Androids Assault Arizona
#17: South Carolina Sea Creatures
#18: Washington Wax Museum
#19: North Dakota Night Dragons
#20: Mutant Mammoths of Montana
#21: Terrifying Toys of Tennessee
#22: Nuclear Jellyfish of New Jersey
#23: Wicked Velociraptors of West Virginia
#24: Haunting in New Hampshire
#25: Mississippi Megalodon
#26: Oklahoma Outbreak
#27: Kentucky Komodo Dragons
#28: Curse of the Connecticut Coyotes
#29: Oregon Oceanauts
#30: Vicious Vacuums of Virginia
#31: The Nevada Nightmare Novel
#32: Idaho Ice Beast
#33: Monster Mosquitoes of Maine
#34: Savage Dinosaurs of South Dakota
#35: Maniac Martians Marooned in Massachusetts
#36: Carnivorous Crickets of Colorado
#37: The Underground Undead of Utah
#38: The Wicked Waterpark of Wyoming
#39: Angry Army Ants Ambush Alabama
#40: Incredible Ivy of Iowa
#41: North Carolina Night Creatures
#42: Arctic Anacondas of Alaska
#43: Robotic Rodents Ravage Rhode Island

great books by Johnathan Rand!

Michigan Chillers:

#1: Mayhem on Mackinac Island
#2: Terror Stalks Traverse City
#3: Poltergeists of Petoskey
#4: Aliens Attack Alpena
#5: Gargoyles of Gaylord
#6: Strange Spirits of St. Ignace
#7: Kreepy Klowns of Kalamazoo
#8: Dinosaurs Destroy Detroit
#9: Sinister Spiders of Saginaw
#10: Mackinaw City Mummies
#11: Great Lakes Ghost Ship
#12: AuSable Alligators
#13: Gruesome Ghouls of Grand Rapids
#14: Bionic Bats of Bay City
#15: Calumet Copper Creatures
#16: Catastrophe in Caseville
#17: A Ghostly Haunting in Grand Haven
#18: Sault Ste. Marie Sea Monsters
#19: Drummond Island Dogman
#20: Lair of the Lansing Leprechauns

Freddie Fernortner, Fearless First Grader:

#1: The Fantastic Flying Bicycle
#2: The Super-Scary Night Thingy
#3: A Haunting We Will Go
#4: Freddie's Dog Walking Service
#5: The Big Box Fort
#6: Mr. Chewy's Big Adventure
#7: The Magical Wading Pool
#8: Chipper's Crazy Carnival
#9: Attack of the Dust Bunnies from Outer Space!
#10: The Pond Monster
#11: Tadpole Trouble
#12: Frankenfreddie
#13: Day of the Dinosaurs

American Chillers Double Thrillers:

Vampire Nation &
Attack of the Monster Venus Melon

Dollar $tore Danny:

#1: The Dangerous Dinosaur
#2: The Salt Shaker Spaceship
#3: The Crazy Crayons
#4: The Shampoo Shark Attack

Adventure Club series:

#1: Ghost in the Graveyard
#2: Ghost in the Grand
#3: The Haunted Schoolhouse

order on line at:
www.americanchillers.com

For Teens:

PANDEMIA: A novel of the
bird flu and the end of the world
(written with Christopher Knight)

USA